T0143936

DAILY HASSLES OF BEING A KID

WRITTEN AND ILLUSTRATED
BY JUSTIN BUCHER

Parents, teachers, and all other grown ups just don't get it!

Hi, my name is Jacob Hayes. I am a normal kid with a pretty normal life. I go through the same things that any other kid my age does. The problem is that our lives as kids would be a whole lot easier if we didn't have to do all the things that grown ups expect us to. For example, think about how much free time that we would have if teachers didn't hand out homework or if they didn't expect us to study for tests. I can think of several other things that I could be doing instead of sitting in my bedroom memorizing my states, learning my math facts, or trying to remember that the letter I goes before E, except after C. The problem is that all adults seem to be in on it. I go to school all day, dealing with teachers, then those same teachers give us homework, and Mom makes me do it. Even the pizza delivery guy reminds me to stay in school, although I am not sure why he says that. Anyway, the bottom line is that it's not fair, and I'm not sure why all grown ups are in on it.

It isn't even just homework. Mom expects me to do different chores around the house too. Doing homework eats into my free time enough, I don't need to have chores added to that pile. Even worse, the chores are responsibilities that I wouldn't even expect my little brother to do. For example, every so often, Mom will go to the basement, take a few steps down the stairs, and say, "**oh, time to change the kitty litter**." Having a cat is great, but there is nothing worse than taking out that horrible, smelly heap of litter when Mom decides the litter needs to be changed.

Not only do we have responsibilities that grown ups expect us to do, they also expect us to **"BEHAVE"** the way that "adults" would. Whatever that means. This problem is 10 times worse while out in public. I've heard Mom's voice get uncontrollably angry more than a couple of times when I may have belched out loud during dinner or even worse out in public at a restaurant. It's interesting to see Mom's face turn from its normal color to beet red in an instant.

The bottom line is... **there has to be a better way**. So, for every hassle, I came up with a solution to fix the problem. There is always a better way, and I think that we, as kids, know better than anyone on how to fix these daily hassles. I think you all agree. Parent's expect us to clean our rooms **WAAAY** too often, and not only that, they have way too many other chores and expectations for us to do too. I am sure that you have your own list of hassles, but these are the hassles that I deal with on a daily basis, and this is how I think that we, as kids, need to fix these hassles.

DAILY HASSLE #1

Cleaning My Bedroom

Mom expects me to clean my room... WAAAY too often.

It's true! Mom's **ALWAYS** telling me to clean my room. Cleaning is the absolute last thing that a kid would ever want to do. Parents know that. There are way too many other things that I could be doing instead of cleaning like playing on my laptop, riding my skateboard, playing video games, or anything else in the world. I think that it would be much easier if Mom could just have my brother do it, or hire a nanny, or program a robot to clean my room! If my room didn't get so messy, it wouldn't be such a problem to clean, but somehow my room does get messy. Even if I do clean my room, a few days later, it's messy all over again. I don't even know how it happens...at least that's what I tell Mom.

I bet that Mom **NEVER** had to clean her room when she was a kid. I bet that she got away with just throwing all of her toys in her closet or just stuffing them under her bed. Her mom probably never even checked to see if her bedroom was clean. Now that she's a Mom, she doesn't let anything slide because of all the tricks that she pulled as a kid. The worst part is Mom expects the room to be spotless; she checks **EVERYTHING**. How's a kid supposed to deal with that? Maybe I should try telling Mom to clean her own room, and see how that goes. Nah, that's not a very good idea. Very bad things could happen.

Something that probably should be brought up, there are a few weird things that seem to be happening in my room that I am kind of scared to go near. I don't think that Mom even knows what is going on in there. First of all, there is an odd smell coming from somewhere in my room, but I can't tell where exactly that stench is coming from. I've only had food in here a couple of times (without Mom knowing of course) but that was over 6 months ago. Come to think of it, I don't remember what I did with that piece of pizza that didn't get eaten in here last month. There is also that strange lump of fuzzy greenish-gray stuff that's growing in my closet. That lump used to be... well, I am not sure what it used to be, but that lump seems to be growing fuzzier every day. I certainly don't think that I should be the one to get that mess out of my closet. Especially, since I can't even tell what it is. That lump of fuzz could be some strange mutation, and if I touch it, that fuzz would instantly infect me and turn me into a **MUTANT-UNDEAD-ZOMBIE** or something. I can picture Mom calling me down for lunch, then me walking right past her with both my arms stretched out in front of me and repeating, **"BRAINS"** over and over again. I don't think that Mom would be very happy if that happened.

If Mom knew about that fuzzy mess, I am sure that she would see it my way, and have a Biohazard Waste Removal Swat Team come get that toxic mess out of my closet. I don't think that Mom has any idea what she is dealing with here. Mom better get that mess cleaned up before there's a major problem, and **EVERYONE** in the house gets turned into zombies, and we all are trying to eat each other's brains.

Not so long ago, I remember Mom cleaning my room for me. I never had to worry about anything back then. Any mess that I made, she would clean up for me. Then one day everything changed... for the worse. When I was way too little to understand, Mom told me to clean up the mess of blocks that I had made all over my bedroom floor. Needless to say, I did what any kid would do, I screamed loud enough for the neighbors down the street to hear. In the end, Mom still made me pick-up every block, and she didn't even help! From that day forward, life has not been same.

The worst part is, the older I get, the more that Mom expects me to clean. Not only am I expected to clean my room now, but I am also expected to clean my mess after breakfast, put away all of my supplies after I get done with a project, clean up the juice that I spilled all over the floor, bring my dirty clothes to the laundry room... the list goes on and on. This seems to be a major problem that needs to have a remedy for me and other kids to have fun being kids while we can.

My fix for the problem.

In my opinion, parents need to figure out how to keep the house clean all on their own. I don't think that it is very smart of Mom to chance having her kids turned into zombies, eating her and the rest of the family's brains. So, I think that it is safest for the whole family to have us kids stay clear of cleaning our rooms or any other cleaning for that matter.

The best option, I think, as I said earlier, my parents should just get a robot that keeps the house clean, does all of the laundry, does all of my chores, and maybe cooks better than Mom. That way, there is no chance of a zombie attack, and we would have a better cook in the house. Mom's cooking is a whole other problem though, but that's how I think this problem should get solved.

DAILY HASSLE #2

Dealing with Substitute Teachers

Dealing with our normal teachers is bad enough, substitute teachers are IMPOSSIBLE.

It's true! Where do these people come from? The stone age? Our substitute teachers have no idea how to handle us kids in the classroom, and what's **HILARIOUS** is their understanding of the technology in the classroom is even worse. The subs spend more time trying to figure out how to use each device for their lesson, than actually using it to teach the class. Not to mention, trying not to lose their cool with the class while fumbling through each problem, which fuels the fun for us kids. This all fuels the frustration for the teacher, which makes for a roller coaster ride all day long.

It's funny how you can see the pain all over the teacher's face when they first peek their head into the classroom. It's clear they know the second they step their foot in that classroom they are doomed and they are going to go home with a monster of a headache at the end of the day.

One of our substitute teachers actually tried using a real permanent marker on the smartboard instead of a smartboard pen. Fortunately, for the sub, my friend, Roger had stopped him before the catastrophe happened. I can't imagine what would have happened if our regular teacher, Ms. Alberson, would have come back to find that her smartboard was covered with permanent marker.

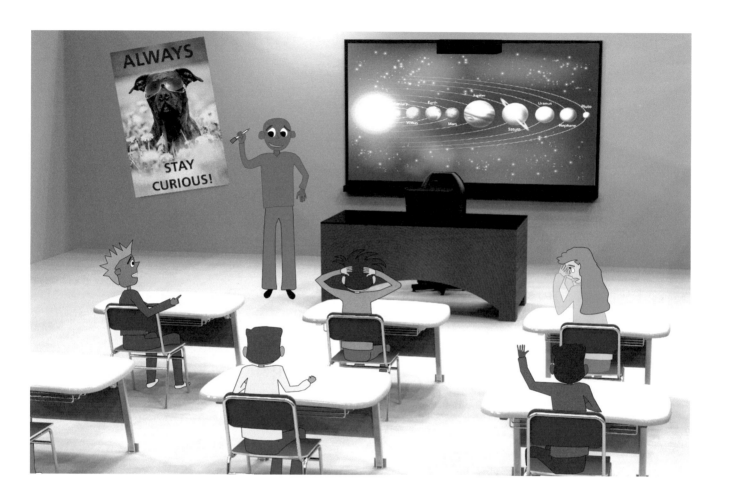

Another sub spent half the class trying to figure out how to turn the smartboard on, then spent nearly the rest of the class trying to find the mouse for the smartboard. Not a single one of us kids dropped the ball and let it slip that you just draw right on the screen with your finger or use the smartboard pen. To say the least, our sub was not happy. I haven't seen her back here since, and that was two years ago.

This is one of the few times that the smart kids can actually find humor in the same things as the rest of us in the class. Of course, we get the whole, "When I was your age," speech from the substitute. They try to explain that they didn't have all of this technology when they were in school, trying to cover up and make excuses for their lack of understanding. They also try taking it from a different angle and explain that they were more respectful to their subs when they were kids. The problem for the sub is that we could not care less what they went through as kids, nor do we want a lecture from them about it. So, the ball keeps rolling and we keep up the fun, and the substitute yet can't figure out what to do to stop this torture.

Aside from the whole technology side, our subs usually don't have a clue about the subjects they are trying to teach the class. It's hilarious to watch a substitute try to teach our class about subjects that they haven't dealt with in twenty years. Some even struggle with basic math principles. Some joke and say that adults just use calculators to do math. You have to wonder how some of these subs made it through school themselves.

For some reason, our subs actually think that we are going to let them know when they are doing something wrong during class. Not even the smart kids want to miss a chance at getting in on the fun when the sub is stumbling through their lesson. Everyone knows having fun and messing with the sub is one of the best parts of having your regular teacher gone.

Only once have we had a sub buckle down and call the principal on us. Kids were throwing paper airplanes, saying rude comments, obviously not listening, and making fun of this sub. This poor substitute teacher was just about in tears. This, I think is worse than a bad report to the teacher. Instead of getting sent to the principal's office, the entire class had the principal come to us, even the smart kids got to have the principal come and have a word with them.

The only problem with all of this is that the entire class knows in the end we are going to lose. We all know the next day when our teacher returns, there is always going to be that horrible note from the sub giving the explicit details of the terrible things that we did the day before. This is one of those extremely rare times when you can see fear in even the smarts kid's faces as our teacher reads out load all of the awful things that happened the day before. In the worst case scenario, if the teacher is really mad, it causes extra homework for us all. All of this does make us think twice about the next time... until the next time our teacher is gone, and we get a new sub. You know you can't help yourself, but do it all over again... even the smart kids can't.

My fix for the problem.

It seriously, seems as though our school finds the subs from online ads. There should be some restrictions for the subs. They should at least know how to operate a smartboard. It would be very helpful if the sub would try to understand that the kids are going to mess with them, and try to have a sense of humor about it. That would make the day go so much smoother for everyone.

DAILY HASSLE #3

Grow-up, show more responsibility, and FESS-UP WHEN I MESS UP.

Now that I am getting older, Mom expects me to act my age and show a bit more responsibility.

I am not even sure what Mom means by that. Just because I don't always behave the way that she expects, doesn't mean that I am not acting my age. Right?!?

There may have been a few times that Mom's had to remind me to quit whining or complaining. Just because she's had to ask me to take out the garbage about twelve times in a half an hour doesn't mean that it won't get done. The problem is that I have difficulty finding time in my busy schedule to get my chores done. My schedule, which includes finding **ANYTHING** to keep myself occupied to buy some time, so I don't have to take out the trash! Mom doesn't understand that I intend to eventually take it out... sometime.

The problem is that when Mom finally gets **FURIOUS** and starts yelling because the full bag of garbage is still sitting in the kitchen, just waiting to go out, whining seems like a completely logical way to react. As a kid, you really don't have any other defense. I don't think that Mom would appreciate it if I explained the possible health hazards of being exposed to noxious rubbish that could potentially negatively affect my well-being or even worse, the entire family's. So, I do what any kid my age would do, procrastinate and complain until Mom flips out and forces me to do it.

Aside from the whole garbage thing, Mom also expects me to clean up after myself, put away anything that I've taken out, and be a responsible role model for my little brother. Whatever that means?!? If I take the cookies out, they have to go right back in the cupboard. Anything I touch now, Mom wants it put away. What is even worse, if my little brother makes a mess, once in a while, Mom will ask me to help him clean it up. **NOW THAT IS TOTALLY UNFAIR!!!!** Right?!? He made the mess. Why should I have to help clean it up? So, again, this seems like a totally logical time to whine and maybe argue with Mom and my brother a bit. Make the point that this was all his fault, not mine. The problem is that I don't remember a single time when Mom has **EVER** sided with me while having this argument, although I have tried several times to make a valid point. It **NEVER** seems to work out in my favor... Maybe I am just doing it wrong?!?

Another item that creates some friction is that Mom has this thing, if, and when something mysteriously happens, like juice gets spilled on the floor or one of her plants gets knocked over, and I am the only one in the room, she automatically assumes that I created the mess. It seems like there could be a slight chance that she might not know who it was, which leaves the opportunity to pin it on my little brother or maybe the dog. The problem is that Mom seems to have this keen sense, she always seems to know when I am not being completely truthful. I don't know how she does it. So, again, in the end, I end up losing. If lying to Mom doesn't really make her go off the deep end. You know makes her completely flip? It's when I belch, and she can hear me from upstairs, down the hall, and two rooms over. She comes storming into the room demanding to know what in the world just came out of me. It is bizarre, and very scary at the same time, to see my loving Mom turn into an **ANGRY MONSTER**. All of this fuss, simply because of a bodily function that I needed to let happen.

One last thing that crabs Mom out, is when my brother and I are playing together, and 5 minutes later, either he or I are running up to Mom tattling about something that the other had done. Then we go back to playing, and a few minutes later the other is tattling to Mom again. Then the other is back up to Mom tattling again, then the other. Usually after this goes on a few more times, Mom blows a gasket, and both of us get to go sit in our rooms quietly for a while. At this point, Mom doesn't care which one of us is to blame. She wants both of us out of her sight to regain her sanity.

Unfortunately, once we are both out of trouble, and we go back to playing, something is going to happen again. One of us is going to tattle, and thus the game begins...let's see who can get the other in the most amount of trouble, more so, we do what we can to get as much trouble off of our own backs. Usually, after this happens for the second time Mom's head swells up and turns beet red until it finally explodes, and once again the angry monster comes out. And once again, both of us are sent to our rooms for quiet time. Sometimes it takes a couple of hours for Mom to degenerate back to her normal self again, so she can come back to each of our rooms and tell us calmly for the umpteenth time why what we did was wrong. I always want to tell Mom, when she comes into my room to talk, that I feel like I am in some sort of 1930's black and white horror movie. I want to tell her how I can actually watch her uncontrollably turn from my sweet, loving mom into a **BIG SCARY MONSTER**. However, I don't think that's a very good idea, especially when I am already in trouble. I know bad things could happen.

My fix for the problem.

Eh... we're just kids. There is no fixing that. Alright, maybe there are few things that I could do to be more responsible and act my age. Maybe I could be more respectful to Mom and try not to belch out loud so often. You know, secretly, I bet even Mom wishes that she could let it out once in a while, and let **EVERYONE** know. The instant gratification is amazing. Thinking about it, you can't help but smile inside.

Alright, maybe I could stop tattling on my brother so much. I know that makes her **CRAZY**. I love Mom; I know that I shouldn't push her buttons so much.

DAILY **H**ASSLE #**4**

Homework

Teachers expect us to do homework...
EVERY SINGLE NIGHT!!

The problem with going to school everyday, isn't just the fact that we have to go to school every day. On top that, our teachers expect us to take our school work home with us, and they expect us to take a lot of it home. Who decided that this was a good idea in the first place?

I would be willing to bet that my teachers get together at school and try to figure out ways to make the student's lives the least fun as possible. That's probably what my teachers do when they go to the Teacher's Lounge. They know that's the only room in the whole school that kids aren't allowed to go in. Well, except for the Janitor's Room... but who wants to go in there? A mob of teachers probably meets in the Teacher's Lounge everyday at lunch time to plan their evil schemes for us kids. I am sure they love to talk about all of the tests, reports, and homework that they are planning for us kids. I bet there's a lot of laughing and giggling going on in that room during their "meetings."

I bet they all get together and discuss different schemes to figure out how to create as much work as possible for the kids in their class. I can picture my

Social Studies teacher, laughing and telling his teacher colleagues about the ten page report that he's going to assign for us, and my Math teacher laughing about the pop-quiz that he is going to give us on Wednesday, then the 4 page test that he is going to throw at us on Friday. And then my English teacher telling everyone about the 20 pages of literature that she is going to make us read over the weekend.

They all probably plan, months in advance, for major projects that they can assign over our breaks. I bet they really enjoy making our vacations seem as short as possible. They probably think, "Ah, spring break is coming. Should I make them write a report? Give them several worksheets to fill their break up? Or, make them read two extra chapters of their book?" I am sure the whole idea of planning different projects for us to do while we are away from school just tickles the teachers pink.

This **ALL** probably makes them laugh and giggle the whole time while having their meeting in the Teacher's Lounge. On the other hand, our teachers try to make excuses about the homework they assign. They try to explain the reasons behind what they do. First, I've had a few teachers tell me that they also have "homework" (teacher homework) to do too. They say that they have papers to grade, tests to grade, they say that they even have to prepare a lesson plan for each class. They go on and on about all the "homework" they have to do. But, I know what their teacher homework really is. They are following through with the plans they made during their "meeting" in the Teacher's Lounge. They're making sure that they don't miss any chance to assign as much work as possible for us kids. Second, my teachers say that when they were kids their teachers assigned homework for them as well. They try to explain that we aren't the only ones that have to do it. However, I bet their teachers took pity on them. I bet their teachers only assigned homework when they had to. Like if the teacher got in trouble with the principal for being too nice and didn't give enough work to the students, and the teachers were told that they had to assign homework. I bet that is the only time that they had homework assigned to them.

One area that I bet my teachers struggle with is what to do with themselves during summer vacation. It's probably pretty tough to spend three months without a single paper to grade or assignment to hand out. On the other hand, they probably have plenty of time to plan for the next school year. They have all summer to figure out the best assignments and projects that will keep us kids working on school work outside of school, instead of having fun during our free time away from there. All of this, I am sure makes the teachers very happy.

My fix for the problem.

I think the school should have rules about teachers giving out homework. I think that the school should give teachers detention for assigning any type of homework at all. I think that teachers should also have their parents called when they get detention, maybe that would take care of the homework problem.

It would be nice if teachers had a bit more compassion for the kids in their class. I would be a lot happier if they didn't have their "meetings" in the Teacher's Lounge anymore, and if they didn't spend their summers planning their students' workload for the following school year. I think they get way too much enjoyment out of seeing us do school work outside of school. All I ask is to have a bit more free time to ourselves during the evening and weekends.

Daily Hassle #5

Getting Up EARLY in the Morning

Grown ups expect us to get up WAAAY too early in the morning to get ready for school.

It's true! If grown ups didn't expect us to get up and go to school so early in the morning, kid's lives would be a whole lot easier. Grown ups expect us to get up and get ready, even though every single one of us would rather stay in bed for several more hours and sleep as long as we wanted. The worst part is not only do we have to get up early, we are getting up early to get ready for **SCHOOL!** How fair is that?!?!

What's equally unfair is that if I am not up after the second snooze, Mom flies in on her broomstick, and makes sure that I do get out of bed. I don't like that at all, especially when I am only half awake.

I don't see the point in getting out of bed, just so I can be hassled by Mom to brush my hair, eat breakfast, brush my teeth, put my homework in my backpack, and get out the door. All of this hassle, just so I can go to school. Maybe, if I was going on a school field trip or something, then maybe I would be a little more excited about getting up in the morning.

Once I'm finally up and getting ready for school, Mom expects me to get everything done on time. If Mom catches me not getting ready, she usually flies right back in on her broomstick, and enforces the rules all over again. Mom doesn't understand that if she allowed me to hit the snooze a few more times, I would be a lot more willing to get out of bed and get ready on time. If I wasn't so tired from getting up right away, I certainly wouldn't be dragging my feet all morning. More importantly, Mom wouldn't have to get her broomstick out.

GET OUT OF BED! GET READY FOR SCHOOL!!

One thing I know that Mom hasn't even considered. If she allowed me to watch cartoons in the morning, I would be a lot more motivated to get out of bed and get ready for school. I bet that if I had the option to watch an hour of cartoons before school every morning, I wouldn't be so crabby with Mom or anyone else in the house. I think that everyone agrees, cartoons are the basis of what mornings are about for kids. Cartoons are the one thing that actually makes **EVERY** kid want to get out of bed. I think that it is important for parents to understand this, and parents should allow cartoons to be a part of every kid's morning routine.

On the other side, not only should parents be more lenient and allow their kids to get up later, parents should also allow us to stay up as late as we want every night. Who wants to go to bed when you can stay up all night and do stuff, like watch TV, play video games, play on the laptop, or do whatever makes us happy? Who wouldn't want to stay up and have online gaming battles against their friends until 2 am? I don't think that it gets any better than that. For some reason, I don't think my parents agree with that point.

My fix for the problem.

If it were up to me, I would say that **NO ONE** should be expected to get up before 8:00 in the morning. If adults asked kids when we want to get up, we would **NOT** answer, **EARLY IN THE MORNING!**

Every kid knows that school should start later in the day and get out earlier in the afternoon. We shouldn't have to deal with early bed times or getting up early in the morning. Kids should have more time to enjoy being a kid.

If we were able to get up later, stay up later, watch cartoons, or do whatever else we wanted, I bet that kids would be a lot more willing to sit through boring classes like History or Math. Listening to your teacher recite historic events or calculating math problems longer than two minutes is enough to put anyone to sleep. So, if classes are going to start early, teachers should at least figure out a way to make the classes easier to sit through.

But, instead, I get to listen to Mom every day hassling me to get out of bed, go to school, and get to bed early. How fun is that for a kid?!?

Daily Hassle #6

Riding the School Bus

Riding the bus shouldn't be this big of a headache!

Literally! It shouldn't be this big of a headache. The seats on the bus are hard as a rock, the bus driver drives like a maniac, and I swear she makes sure to hit every bump. Which, as fast as she goes, I am surprised that we don't go airborne off some of those bumps.

Gertrude, our bus driver, really seems to enjoy watching us kids squirm while she's driving. She says that we behave better when we're scared. I guess Gertrude's had a few too many spit wads shot in the back of her head in the past. I think, on the other hand, that she should be more understanding, and at least try to miss a few of the pot holes now and then.

The other problem with having such a bumpy ride is that it's almost impossible to get my homework done that I didn't finish the night before. There is always that last little bit that you tell yourself, "I'll just finish this tomorrow on the bus." But, once you're on the bus it's **ALWAYS** impossible to get done. The other problem is that the work that does get done has, what my teachers call, "**BUS HANDWRITING**." They say the writing is "**ILLEGIBLE**"... whatever that means. This is because at every bump, stop, turn, or change in motion, my pencil jerks when I am trying to write. My teachers have complained before about bus handwriting, and some say that they won't take work that they can't read. In my defense, if my bus driver wasn't such a maniac driver, I wouldn't have a problem with bus handwriting.

Aside from the whole bus handwriting problem, something that has been wreaking havoc on the bus the past few weeks is that Gertrude got a brand new intercom system installed on her bus. So, now when even a minor problem occurs, Gertrude jumps on that intercom, and we all get to listen to her angry voice 10 times louder over the four newly installed speakers throughout the bus. I swear Gertrude is just trying to get back at us for all of the trouble that we've caused her throughout the years. We all know that we have put her through a lot, **BUT THIS JUST ISN'T FAIR!** Every little thing that happens, Gertrude's voice comes boasting over the speakers.

One day, my friend Charlie was just trying to show off his grade that he was so proud of on his report that he handed in last week. He only had his paper out and was showing it off for a few minutes before the bus driver jumped on her intercom and started yelling, **"SIT DOWN! NO TALKING ON THE BUS!"** Poor Charlie must have been so upset and embarrassed. He was so proud of the grade that he had gotten. He boasted that he had worked on that report for at least an hour, but I think that he was probably exaggerating.

The problem is that we didn't even do anything wrong, and we still got in trouble. Something has got to be done to put a **STOP** to this madness.

Aside from that whole issue, something else that all the kids know is taboo is falling asleep on the bus. It has been known that when someone falls asleep, really bad things happen to that kid. I certainly don't want to be one of those unlucky kids who wake-up full of spit wads, covered in permanent marker, or even worse find that I didn't make it off the bus when we got to school. I know a kid who fell asleep once, got covered with black permanent marker, and not only did he have to spend the rest of the day at school like that... the marker didn't fully disappear for a week! This incident happened about three years ago, and to this day he is still called, "Parker the Permanent Marker." I am sure he'll be called that at his 20 year class reunion. All of this fuss, just because he fell asleep on the bus one day. That is not a legacy that I would want to be stuck with for the rest of my life.

My fix for the problem.

The best case scenario would be to get a different bus driver, one who actually enjoys being around kids. What a dream that would be! Maybe get a bus driver that has a valid driver's license and didn't drive like a maniac. At least get rid of that **AWFUL** intercom. That, alone, would make the trip to school much easier to handle. I don't enjoy starting my day getting screamed at by Gertrude. Maybe Gertrude would benefit from visiting our school counselor to figure out how to handle her anger issues. She could take that rage and turn it around, and figure out how to use that energy on a more positive level. Wait a minute, that didn't just come out of **MY** mouth, did it? Anyway, our bus driver needs help!

DAILY HASSLE #7

Getting Dressed-up for Special Occasions

I don't think there has ever been a kid that actually wanted to get dressed-up for any occasion... EVER!!!

I don't understand why parents do this to us. Making me put on a suit and tie, for any occasion, is worse than any punishment that my parents could dish out. I often wonder if my parents remember what it was like when they were kids. I can't imagine that things were any different for them when they were forced to get dressed-up. So, why would they torture us the same way? It makes no sense. The embarrassment and discomfort that parents put us through is, well, crazy! On top of that, parents are just asking for trouble when they let us run around doing what kids do best, ruin stuff. They know it is just a matter of time before something happens like a grass stain, grape juice spills, or whatever. But the end result is that even though we would give anything not to wear a suit, we are still in serious trouble when something goes wrong, and the outfit gets ruined. How fair is that?!?

Besides looking and feeling completely ridiculous in a suit and tie, the clothes are extremely uncomfortable. Starting with shoes that I've put on for the first time in my life. They are beyond stiff and have zero forgiveness to them. Mom had ironed my shirt and pants, and both are equally as stiff and uncomfortable as the shoes. Then, Mom makes me put a suit jacket on top of all of that, and not only am I uncomfortable from the stiff clothes, now I am dying of heat because of the jacket that I have to wear in an overly warm room. Who in their right mind thought that it was a good idea to put kids through this?

Then, there was that wedding that Mom and Dad made us kids go to last year. The worst part wasn't sitting through the wedding ceremony. It was once it was over, and anyone and everyone had come up to pinch my cheeks and comment on how **ADORABLE** I looked in my suit. Mom and Dad were so proud of their "little boy;" **I HAVE NEVER BEEN SO EMBARRASSED IN MY LIFE**!! This type of torture is just cruel and unusual. I would be willing to bet that this kind of torture was used in the dark ages. They probably embarrassed people by forcing them to dress-up in suits and ties, and had old people lined up to pinch their cheeks and comment on how adorable they looked. I can't imagine anything worse happening to anyone.

Not only do I have to deal with everyone else pinching my cheeks and listen to their annoying comments. I also have to watch my every move when I am dressed-up. Mom expects me to behave in my nice clothes. She expects me to act like a, "gentleman" as Mom puts it. Which means that acting like any kid my age is out of the question. There is no such thing as going outside and playing like any normal kid would do. Mom expects me to be on my best behavior, and do everything that I can to not mess up and ruin my nice clothes... **THE NICE CLOTHES I WISH THAT I DIDN'T HAVE TO WEAR IN THE FIRST PLACE!** What fun is that?!?

I can't imagine the extreme trouble that I would be in if I showed up at the end of the night to meet Mom and Dad with a stained suit coat, holes ripped through my pants, and wearing my typical sneakers instead of the dress shoes that they specifically bought to go with this outfit. Mom would absolutely flip-out and do something out of control, like ground me from anything and everything that has any value to me for the rest of life, at least my life while living at home with her and Dad. All over one event that I would have given anything to just stay at home with a sitter instead of attending.

My fix for the problem.

If parents want to get dressed-up for special occasions, they can do what they want, but leave us kids out of it. It's not in a kid's nature to want to act in a non-kid-like manner when dressed-up. Parents know it is inevitable that something bad is going to happen to the special outfit they picked out just for that occasion, and of course it is **ALWAYS** the kid's fault when things go wrong and their stuff gets ruined. Kids are just who they are... kids, we ruin stuff. We can't help it that things just seem to drop and spill on our clothes for no apparent reason.

Parents seem to get extra crabby when they have to dish out a lot when either returning the rented clothes or if the clothes are bought, then settling for us **NEVER** wearing that outfit again. That seems to be the time when either the lecture comes or anything important to me gets taken away.

The bottom line, parents should just let kids wear whatever they are comfortable in. If the outfit gets ruined at the occasion, then that is how it is. That kind of stuff just happens, and we shouldn't get blamed. We are who we are... kids. We ruin stuff, and that will **NEVER, EVER** change. Parents simply need to accept that, and stop getting so cranked when things don't go as planned.

DAILY HASSLE #8

Taking Care of the Family Pets

Oscar and Boomer are great pets, but I had no idea what I had agreed to before we had gotten them.

I think it's great. Mom and Dad agree that we need a few pets running around the house to complete our family. We all love Boomer, our dog, and Oscar, our cat. All of our pets are awesome, but they all have their own quirks.

For some reason, Mom says that just because I was the one who wanted Oscar and Boomer, it is my responsibility to take care of them. Once Mom and Dad agreed to getting them, I of course jumped out of my chair, and assured them that I would absolutely take care of both pets no matter what. For some reason, you only think of the fun side of your pet while you are begging for one. However, I had no idea what I was getting into while agreeing to Mom's terms and conditions.

What's funny is that not only does Mom have rules, Oscar laid one down right after he moved in. He assured us that he expects to have his litter box changed every week, no questions asked, or we get a very unwanted surprise once his litter box is full. So, of course I do what Oscar says and what Mom enforces, I reluctantly change his litter box for him every week. The problem is that Oscar's litter box is the only place in the whole house that I am scared to go near. His litter box is in the basement in its own designated room. It is important to take every necessary precaution when entering this room due to Oscar's hazardous waste and the obnoxious fumes that fill the room. This room should be treated as a toxic waste zone; a gas mask should be required at all times when changing the litter box. That is about the only way that this job would be tolerable. It is really bizarre to me how such an adorable family pet could create such an obnoxious smell.

Aside from that whole matter, Oscar expects to have his food dish full at all times, otherwise he does everything he can to make sure that everyone in the house knows that his bowl is empty. Oscar will meow endlessly and rub against us until someone stops what they are doing and fills his dish. Until this task is done, Oscar makes sure that one of us trips over him by walking between our legs. He doesn't care if someone has their arms full of groceries, or if they are laying down taking a nap. He shows no mercy when it comes to his food. He makes sure that his bowl is full at all times.

Along those same lines, Oscar makes sure that poor Scooter, our fish, lives in terror. Still dreaming of food, Oscar likes to sit in front of Scooter's aquarium and watch him swim back and forth for hours on end. I can't imagine the horror that poor fish goes through. Oscar incessantly paws at the glass as if he is going to somehow get in there and get that fish out. It must be very stressful having someone outside your home at all times longing to have you in their belly.

What I find incredibly funny, on the other hand, is that Boomer plays the same game with Oscar. Boomer chases that cat from room to room, while Oscar flees for his life. Boomer will actually sit and wait patiently for Oscar to come his way. When Oscar is least expecting, Boomer will strike, leaving a frenzy of furious kitty noises, Oscar scrambling to get away, and Boomer having the time of his life. I also find it funny that Oscar doesn't realize that he's torturing poor Scooter the same way when he's batting at his tank.

As long we are on the subject of Boomer, he has a few quirks of his own. After Boomer gets good and wore out from chasing the cat all over the house, he enjoys taking a rest and heading to the toilet to get a nice long, refreshing drink. After which, he is quite happy, and would be more than willing to give a ton of kisses to anyone who is available. I think that everyone in the household agrees that this habit is well... yuuchkk, and we all think twice before letting Boomer lick us, no matter what.

Another problem that Boomer's got is that he seems to think that the couch is **HIS** own napping spot. He likes to sprawl out on the couch, taking just

about the entire thing up. It's almost impossible to sit down and enjoy a movie with the dog sitting in the middle of the couch, kicking and twitching from time to time, not to mention snoring all the while that he is napping. You would think that Boomer would take a hint with everyone nudging and elbowing him, urging him to get off of the couch. He blissfully lays there, though, insisting that is **HIS** spot, and we should take the floor. Now that just isn't fair!

My fix for the problem.

I don't think there is much that you can do about your pet's habits. They are who they are. I just wish they all got along better, and Oscar didn't expect his dish to be full **ALL** of the time. Both Oscar and Boomer have great personalities, so I can deal with a few quirks that each of them has. Although it would be nice if we could break Boomer's habit of drinking out of the toilet.

Copyright © 2015 Justin Bucher.

All rights reserved. No part of this book may be used or reproduced by any means, graphic, electronic, or mechanical, including photocopying, recording, taping or by any information storage retrieval system without the written permission of the publisher except in the case of brief quotations embodied in critical articles and reviews.

Archway Publishing books may be ordered through booksellers or by contacting:

Archway Publishing
1663 Liberty Drive
Bloomington, IN 47403
www.archwaypublishing.com
1 (888) 242-5904

Because of the dynamic nature of the Internet, any web addresses or links contained in this book may have changed since publication and may no longer be valid. The views expressed in this work are solely those of the author and do not necessarily reflect the views of the publisher, and the publisher hereby disclaims any responsibility for them.

Any people depicted in stock imagery provided by Thinkstock are models, and such images are being used for illustrative purposes only. Certain stock imagery © Thinkstock.

ISBN: 978-1-4808-1933-7 (sc)
ISBN: 978-1-4808-1934-4 (e)

Print information available on the last page.

Archway Publishing rev. date: 8/10/2015

Printed in the United States
By Bookmasters